TRAFFIC JAM

BY GEORGE MENDOZA · ILLUSTRATIONS BY DAVID STOLTZ

STEWART, TABORI & CHANG

NEW YORK

Text copyright©1990 George Mendoza
Illustrations copyright©1990 David Stoltz
Design by Joseph Rutt

Published in 1990 by
Stewart, Tabori & Chang, Inc.
740 Broadway, New York, New York 10003

Library of Congress Cataloging-in-Publication Data
Mendoza, George.
      Traffic jam / by George Mendoza : illustrations by David Stoltz.
          p.   cm.
      Summary: Out for a drive, a family finds itself in a traffic jam
created by animals.
      ISBN 1-55670-135-7
      [1. Traffic congestion—Fiction.   2. Automobile driving—Fiction.
3. Animals—Fiction.   4. Stories in rhyme.]   I. Stoltz, David, ill.
II. Title.
PZ8.3.M55164Tr   1990   89-28597
[E]—dc20   CIP
                                                   AC
                                                   Rev.

Distributed in the U.S. by Workman Publishing,
708 Broadway, New York, New York 10003
Distributed in Canada by Canadian Manda Group,
P.O. Box 920 Station U, Toronto, Ontario M8Z 5P9
Distributed in all other territories by
Little, Brown and Company, International Division,
34 Beacon Street, Boston, Massachusetts 02108

Printed in Japan
10 9 8 7 6 5 4 3 2 1

To my friend, Toshio Ohmori
G. M.

For Louise, Barbara & Alexi
D. S.

We all piled in the car one day
to drive to someplace far away.
All the animals joined us too—
my parents thought it was a zoo!

"Oh, dear, we're in a traffic muss,"
Said Mom to Dad and Dad to us.
Out on the streets, the freeways, and byways,
lizards and leopards were jamming the highways.

Right next door I saw a taxi,
on its roof sat blue chimpanzees!

A rhino rode a roller skate.
Said Dad to Mom, "We're running late."

Out my window pigs looked smart, riding in a duck-drawn cart.

If I could drive this silly car,
I'd really drive it very far.

I'd go as fast as police cars go
—with sirens screaming—
CAN'T GO SLOW!

If I were driving that old bus,
I'd give a ride to an octopus.

Lions in limos, I'd drive right through;

they rule the jungle and this zoo too.

I'd steer a truck all through the night:

the stars would make the highway bright.

And when I got to outer space,
I'd hold an intergalactic race.

Back on the road, the sun's gone down.

"Oh, dear," says Mom, "we're still in town."

If I could drive, I'd show them how.
If I could drive, we'd be there now.

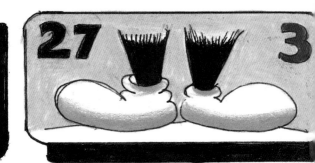

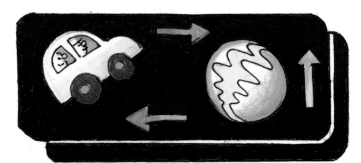